This book belongs to

....

First American Edition 2023
Kane Miller, A Division of EDC Publishing

Text copyright © Macmillan Children's Books 2022
Illustrations copyright © Alberta Torres 2022
The right of Alberta Torres to be identified as the illustrator
of this work has been asserted.
Published under licence from Macmillan Children's Books, a division of
Macmillan Publishers International Limited, London, United Kingdom

For information contact:
Kane Miller, A Division of EDC Publishing
5402 S 122nd E Ave, Tulsa, OK 74146
www.kanemiller.com

Library of Congress Control Number: 2022945265
Printed and bound in China
1 2 3 4 5 6 7 8 9 10

ISBN: 978-1-68464-577-0

MIX
Paper from
responsible sources
FSC® C116313
FSC
www.fsc.org

This Little DINOSAUR

Coral Byers

Alberta Torres

Kane Miller
A DIVISION OF EDC PUBLISHING

This little dinosaur stamps and stomps.

This little dinosaur
swoops and **soars.**

2

This little dinosaur
swirls and **twirls**.

3

And this little dinosaur
ROARS!

4

This little dinosaur
wants to hide.

5

This little dinosaur
plays along.

6

This little dinosaur
counts to ten . . .

Where have all the
dinosaurs gone?

7

This little dinosaur's busy building.

This little dinosaur
wants to play!

This little dinosaur
hears a noise…

KABOOM!

They all run away!

10

And all the little dinosaurs go...

Reading Together
Tips for Parents and Caregivers

This book has been specially created and developed for preschool children. It uses the popular nursery rhyme *This Little Piggy* to create an instantly familiar, read-aloud preschool adventure!

- The fun, repetitive, and rhythmic text helps develop language and vocabulary.

- The bar along the bottom counts from 1 to 10, with numbers on each page to help children recognize numerals.

- The characters in this book are in a preschool classroom. This can help children get used to—and excited about—starting formal childcare or preschool themselves.

- There is plenty of evidence to show that sharing books and reading together helps children to communicate, develop ideas and understanding, and gives them a head start at school. But the most important thing is to enjoy the closeness of sharing a book together.

When you read this book together, you could talk to your child about...

...the ten children in the book. Can your child find and count each one as you go along? **What is each child doing?** You could encourage your child to join in and mimic the children's actions.

...how the children's world changes into **an imaginative, make-believe world** as they play. What can your child see change as they turn the pages?

...things around you that your child could use to **create their own make-believe world.** What would they like to dress up as?

...the numbers in the book—can they find and **read each number?** Try reading the book while your child counts each little dinosaur on their fingers or toes, just like in the nursery rhyme.

Say Hello to the Dinosaurs!

1 **Max** always wants to be first!

2 **Iris** loves to dance.

3 **Aisha** can count all the way to 100!

4 **Muhammed** can shout really loudly!

5 **Grace** loves to play hide-and-seek.

6 **Benjamin** is really good at jumping high.

7 **Noa**'s favorite color is blue.

8 **Evie** likes to play soccer and go swimming.

9 **Ezra**'s favorite food is cake.

10 **Felix** loves to build tall towers.

What will they all dress up as next?